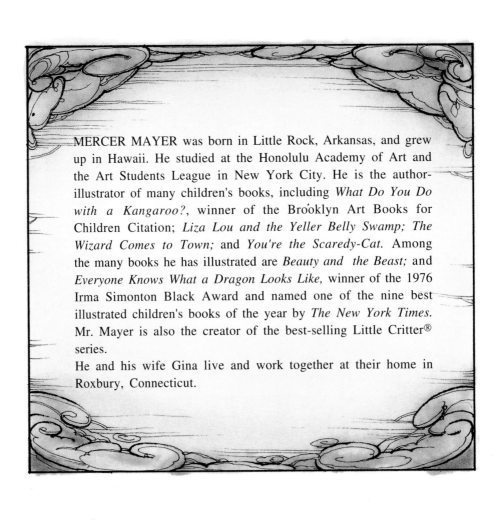

MERCER MAYER was born in Little Rock, Arkansas, and grew up in Hawaii. He studied at the Honolulu Academy of Art and the Art Students League in New York City. He is the author-illustrator of many children's books, including *What Do You Do with a Kangaroo?*, winner of the Brooklyn Art Books for Children Citation; *Liza Lou and the Yeller Belly Swamp; The Wizard Comes to Town;* and *You're the Scaredy-Cat.* Among the many books he has illustrated are *Beauty and the Beast;* and *Everyone Knows What a Dragon Looks Like,* winner of the 1976 Irma Simonton Black Award and named one of the nine best illustrated children's books of the year by *The New York Times.* Mr. Mayer is also the creator of the best-selling Little Critter® series.

He and his wife Gina live and work together at their home in Roxbury, Connecticut.

For Katie Molles

A RAINBIRD BOOK

Packaged by John Sansevere

Library of Congress Catalog Card Number: 80-16784
ISBN: 1-879920-02-6

First **RAINBIRD** Edition 1991
Printed in Italy
Distributed by Publishers Group West

Once I had a silly thought
while sitting in the shade.

What if I'm not me.
Perhaps I am a rock,
a dog, or a tree,
thinking I am me...
What a silly thought.

I laughed so hard I fell
right down and then
I thought some more.

Perhaps each time
I smell a flower,
it is smelling me right back.

Perhaps I'm not where
I think I am.
Where else can I be?
Sitting in a tree?

Or hiding underneath a stone.

And what if I'm floating
high up in the air
and I only think that
I am sitting in the shade.

Perhaps up is down and
down is up and I only
think it's down.

That silly thinking
made me hungry
so I went home to eat.

My dinner lay there
on the plate,
looking up at me.
Then I had a silly thought.

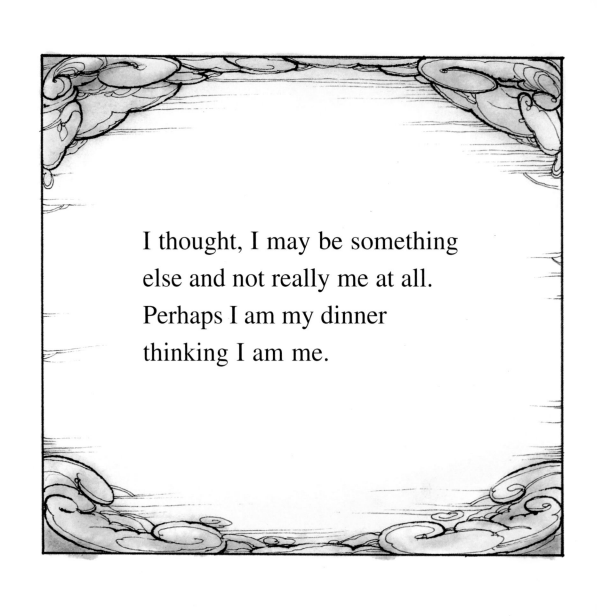

I thought, I may be something
else and not really me at all.
Perhaps I am my dinner
thinking I am me.

That made me laugh
so very hard
I fell right off my chair.

"Eat your dinner,"
my father said.
"Why must you be so silly?"

Maybe I'm not here at all.

Where else can I be?

Perhaps I'm under the tablecloth.

And I just don't know

I'm there.

"Stop that now,"
my mother said,
"and go upstairs to bed."

I put on my pajamas
and crawled into my bed.
Before I knew what happened
I had a silly thought.

Perhaps I am my pillow
and my pillow
is really me.

That made me laugh
so very hard
I fell right out of bed.

Perhaps I'm underneath
the bed,
thinking I'm on top.

All those silly thoughts
running through my head
made me very tired
so I closed my eyes.
While I had my eyes closed
I had a silly thought.

I don't remember
what it was because
I fell asleep.